# I'D RATHER BE WITH A REAL MOM WHO LOVES ME

## A Story for Foster Children

Michael Gordon, Ph.D.
Professor, Department of Psychiatry
Director, Attention Deficit Hyperactivity Disorders Program
State University of New York Health Science Center at Syracuse

Illustrations and design
Janet Junco

**GSI Publications, Inc.**
P.O. Box 746, DeWitt, New York 13214-0746
Phone: (315) 446-4849
Fax: (315) 446-2012

PUBLICATIONS, INC.

Special thanks to Drs. Wendy Gordon, Martin Irwin, and Ronald Saletsky for their comments on the manuscript. I also benefited tremendously from the input of Mr. Frederick DuFour and of Ms. Diane Erné, Deputy Commissioner for Children's Services for the Department of Social Services of Onondaga County, NY.

ISBN 0 -9627701 -8 -3

**GSI Publications, Inc.**
P.O. Box 746, DeWitt, New York 13214-0746
Phone: (315) 446-4849
Fax: (315) 446-2012

**GSI**
PUBLICATIONS, INC.

# To the adult reading this book along with a foster child:

I wrote this book out of frustration with the lack of materials designed to help children deal with their separation from their families. Few life experiences are as devastating to youngsters as being removed from their homes and placed in unfamiliar settings. The circumstances that lead to removal are themselves often terrifying, destructive, and depressing. They leave a child feeling helpless and saddle him or her with sometimes overwhelming rage, guilt, anxiety, and sadness.

Yet too often those of us involved in the care of foster children pay scant attention to their emotional lives. Perhaps because those emotions can be so intense and unpleasant, we are afraid to explore them with children for fear that we'll set off an eruption. Maybe it's just that so much of our time is spent attending to the logistics of the placement or trying to avoid turf battles with other professionals. Regardless of the reasons, youngsters are frequently left alone to cope with the turmoil. Emotional concerns are usually broached only after they have provoked problem behavior.

My general recommendation is to consider reading this book to children placed in foster care even if they are not currently exhibiting obvious distress. By sheer dint of their placement, youngsters will likely identify with at least some of the issues expressed by the little boy in this story.

You'll find that some children won't seem to respond at all to this story, while others will demonstrate interest or discomfort. Of course, you'll have to use your judgment regarding how far to prod the child to talk about the story. Many children will benefit from simply reading this book and discussing it later, usually after they've had a chance to digest the information.

If nothing else, by reading this book you will be communicating important messages to the foster child. First, you'll be making it clear that many of the thoughts and feelings he or she experiences are normal rather than odd or shameful. You'll also be demonstrating your interest in promoting an atmosphere of sensitivity to his or her emotional needs. For children whose lives are so disrupted and sad, a chance to talk about feelings with an understanding and patient adult can set a tone of warmth and hope.

Excuse me for saying so but my life sucks. I'm not supposed to talk nasty but, I'm sorry, my life really sucks.

I don't mean how things are every day. Actually, it's not so terrible in this new foster home. My foster mother's nice. She's patient with me and a couple of the kids here are OK. There are just too many of them running around. And some of them are way more messed up than I am. This one boy Justin is so hyper he can barely sit still and this girl Rachel spends most of the time in the corner crying and rocking, just crying and rocking.

But it's not bad here. It's a lot better than the hellhole foster home I just left. I can't even tell you what happened there. The nicest home was the first one but, like most things in my life, it didn't work out.

My life sucks because nothing's gone right. Foster mothers try to be kind, but I'd rather be with a real mom who loves me.

The thing is that I'm not sure how my life came to suck. My memory of when I was a baby is just a dark cloud. I remember dirt and being hungry and lots of screaming. I remember being confused, and sleeping in strange places, and never knowing what was going to happen next.

Then I remember my mom being drunk, and being gone, and then coming home but acting weird. I remember a man who might have been my father and a man who was scary and a man who did things I don't want to talk about.

4

I remember my grandparents taking me away and then I remember being put in the first foster home. But more than the details, I remember being frightened and worried about my mother, and wondering why someone couldn't love me and protect me from bad things.

My case worker's nice enough. But why doesn't she tell me what's going to happen before it happens? She's got this idea that I'll get upset if she gives me some warning that I have to go to a new home or that my mother won't show up for a visitation. Well, sure I'll get upset, but not as much as when, bam, I'm told, "Pack up your things. We need to move you to another home." Not that it takes that long to gather my stuff.

That's why I say my life sucks. People take control over me and I don't have any say. I never feel comfortable because in the back of my mind I'm thinking, "Don't get too happy because any minute now something bad's gonna happen." I never can feel that life's OK.

Can you believe they expect me to do well in school?
I know I should get good grades, but my mind always
wanders to thoughts of my mother, or to my little sister
who lives with my grandparents, or to just how I'd rather
be with a real mom who loves me. And how about a dad
who could act like a dad?

It's hard to pay attention to math problems when you get as worried or sad as I do. When I try to get work done, I get so frustrated. Or I'll get upset at dumb things another kid might say. This anger inside of me comes from nowhere and sweeps me away like a tornado. I'll run off or hit somebody or do something mean. Or get myself thrown out of one foster home and into another. Half the time I'm not quite sure what set me off other than this feeling of being out of control and miserable and wanting someone to make the ugliness go away.

Here's the thing that sucks most about my sucky life: I feel like I have to choose sides between my foster family and my birth family. When I start getting close to my foster mom and dad, then a part of me feels like I'm hurting my mom. And if I begin to get close to my mom, then I feel bad for my foster parents who, after all, are the ones who take care of me.

It doesn't help much that the case worker makes me call both my foster mother and my birth mother "Mom." It would be easier if I could call Gladys just Gladys and save "Mom" for Mom. Don't tell anyone, but I like the idea of saving "Mom" for a real mom who loves me. I'm just afraid that she might not be my birth mother . . . but you never know.

The adults have it in their mind that all will be well if I just get enough help from doctors. I spend most of my life going from one therapist to another. It's too bad they don't give frequent flyer miles for taxi cab rides. The thing is that I go to so many different people that I miss lots of school and rarely have an afternoon to play.

"SO, HOW DOES THAT MAKE YOU FEEL?"

"AND HOW DOES THAT MAKE YOU FEEL?"

"HOW DOES THAT MAKE YOU FEEL?"

"SO, MAN-LIKE- HOW DOES THAT -LIKE- MAKE YOU FEEL?"

Don't get me wrong. Most of the therapists have tried hard, and I can't say it hasn't helped to talk to someone. But you want to know the truth? They have this idea that I'll get better if I talk endlessly about my feelings. They're always asking, "How does that make you feel?" when most of the time I'd rather just be with someone who's nice and let's me talk when I'm good and ready to talk. A lot of my feelings are scary and I'd rather leave them be. And some things I'm simply not ready to talk about.

"HOW DOES THAT MAKE YOU FEEL?"

"AND SO HOW DOES THAT MAKE YOU FEEL?"

"AND HOW DOES THAT MAKE YOU FEEL?"

"AND THAT MAKES YOU FEEL.... WHAT?"

13

So maybe I should get a t-shirt to wear to my appointments that says, "Wanna know how I feel? Life sucks."

14

What helps most is when they explain things to me I'm confused about. It takes me awhile, but I usually let them know when something upsets me.

Like the other day I got it into my head that I was going to get AIDS because one of my weird foster brothers spit into my glass. The psychologist at school explained that I was safe. I trust him enough so I could relax about it.

Although I haven't gotten too close to most of the therapists, I do like this one lady, Dr. Lee. She plays games and talks like the others, but she has a big mouth when she thinks people are doing dumb things to me. She looks out for me and causes all kinds of trouble if she's not happy with what's going on. I like that in a therapist. She also doesn't try to hide things from me. She answers my questions and she's straight with me—even if I don't always want to hear what she's got to say.

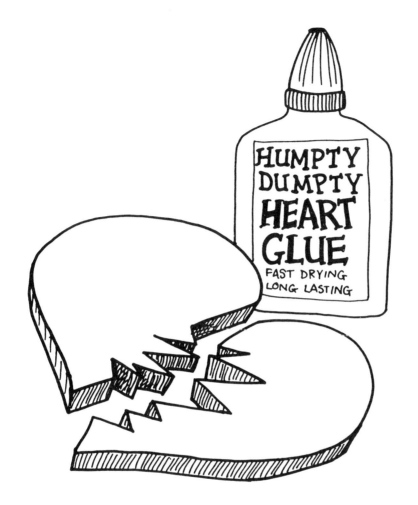

What's hardest for me is to trust anyone. Even Dr. Lee. Every time I start to feel close to her, this fear comes over me that I'll lose her like I've lost so many others. It's hard to explain, but I sorta have to run away from people before we get close. I'd rather keep my distance than have to deal with any more broken hearts.

So half the time I want people to love me and the other half I'm keeping people who want to love me far away. Not listening, cursing, and acting cold are my major weapons against others getting too close. The sad thing is that people get turned off when I'm mean and they stop trying to help me.

18

I finally got the guts to ask Dr. Lee what I could do to feel better about my life. Like most of these therapists, she didn't come out and tell me exactly what to do. We kinda worked it out together. We made a list of what would help me.

The first thing on the list was that I should learn to tell someone I trust when I'm confused or upset. We decided it would be a good idea if I could let someone know with words and not by losing control.

But the big thing I've got to get through my thick skull is that it's not my fault how things have worked out. Especially stuff about my mother. I just think about her or see some other mom with her kid and I feel like I'm sinking into a black hole. I can't stop thinking that we could be together if I took better care of her or if I were a better kid or if I had done something different. If I'm not feeling guilty, I feel so angry toward her that you can't begin to imagine. She should have taken care of me.

Some kids seem to make it through OK and others fall apart. Now Jeremy, this counselor at summer camp, he had an even tougher time than me, but he says he's happy now. He told me it took him a long time before he got it together. I think he said something about getting tired of being angry and deciding to take control of his life. He got into karate, too. But most of all he got adopted by a decent family. It must be nice to find a mother who really loves you.

Angela, this girl at school, was also a foster kid. She ended up going back home when her mother got her act together and could take care of her. It sounds like it took years for things to settle down. But they did.

I hope I didn't make you sad by telling this story. It's funny, though. I feel better telling you what goes on with me, even though we've never met and probably never will.

All I can say is that I don't think I'm the only one whose life sucks. Maybe some of this stuff happened to you. Well, you're not alone, trust me. Somebody should tell parents everywhere that all kids need a real mom and dad who love them.

**To order** one of Dr. Gordon's books or for more information, just complete the order form and mail it back to us.

Name: _____

Street: _____

City: _____ State: _____ Zip: _____

❏ **ADHD / Hyperactivity:** A Consumer's Guide For Parents and Teachers ........................**$14.95**

❏ **Jumpin' Johnny Get Back to Work!** A Child's Guide to ADHD/Hyperactivity ................**$10.00**

❏ **Jumpin' Johnny Video & Book Set** Set including VHS Video & Complete Book ....................**$45.00**

❏ **Juanito Saltarín ¡A Tu Trabajo De Nuevo!** Spanish version of 'Jumpin Johnny'............**$11.00**

❏ **I Would If I Could:** A Teenager's Guide To ADHD/Hyperactivity......................................**$12.50**

❏ **My Brother's a World Class Pain** A Sibling's Guide to ADHD/Hyperactivity................**$11.00**

❏ **I'd Rather Be With A Real Mom Who Loves Me** A story for Foster Children.................**$12.00**

❏ **Teaching the Child With Attention Deficit Disorder** A Slide Program for
In-Service Teacher Training ..................................................................................................**$150.00**

❏ **How to Operate an ADHD Clinic or Subspecialty Practice** A treasure trove
of guidelines, concepts, practicalities, insights, cautions, observations, state-of-the art
research, and clinic-spun humor ..........................................................................................**$59.95**

❏ **Publications Brochure** Contains complete descriptions of all our books and
ordering information ..............................................................................................................**Free**

| | |
|---|---|
| If your order is for an address outside the Continental U.S. or Canada, or an APO or FPO address, please call us for the shipping charges | **Sub Total:** _____ <br> **Add 10%** to your order for shipping: _____ <br> **Add 20%** to your order for shipping to Canada: _____ <br> (N.Y.S. residents add 7% tax): _____ <br> **Total:** _____ |

❏ Check enclosed, payable to GSI Publications
❏ Mastercard  ❏ Visa    Expiration Date:_____
Card Number:_____

_____
Cardholder's Signature

**GSI Publications, Inc.**
P.O. Box 746, DeWitt, New York 13214-0746
Phone: (315) 446-4849
Fax: (315) 446-2012

Call us for quantity discounts on large orders.

PUBLICATIONS, INC.

**To order** one of Dr. Gordon's books or for more information, just complete the order form and mail it back to us.

Name: _____

Street: _____

City: _____ State: _____ Zip: _____

☐ **ADHD / Hyperactivity:** A Consumer's Guide For Parents and Teachers .........................$14.95
☐ **Jumpin' Johnny Get Back to Work!** A Child's Guide to ADHD/Hyperactivity ................$10.00
☐ **Jumpin' Johnny Video & Book Set** Set including VHS Video & Complete Book ...................$45.00
☐ **Juanito Saltarín ¡A Tu Trabajo De Nuevo!** Spanish version of 'Jumpin Johnny'............$11.00
☐ **I Would If I Could:** A Teenager's Guide To ADHD/Hyperactivity..................................$12.50
☐ **My Brother's a World Class Pain** A Sibling's Guide to ADHD/Hyperactivity................$11.00
☐ **I'd Rather Be With A Real Mom Who Loves Me** A story for Foster Children.................$12.00
☐ **Teaching the Child With Attention Deficit Disorder** A Slide Program for
   In-Service Teacher Training ........................................................................................$150.00
☐ **How to Operate an ADHD Clinic or Subspecialty Practice** A treasure trove
   of guidelines, concepts, practicalities, insights, cautions, observations, state-of-the art
   research, and clinic-spun humor ..................................................................................$59.95
☐ **Publications Brochure** Contains complete descriptions of all our books and
   ordering information ...................................................................................................**Free**

| | |
|---|---|
| If your order is for an address outside the Continental U.S. or Canada, or an APO or FPO address, please call us for the shipping charges | **Sub Total:** _____ <br> **Add 10%** to your order for shipping: _____ <br> **Add 20%** to your order for shipping to Canada: _____ <br> (N.Y.S. residents add 7% tax): _____ <br> **Total:** _____ |

☐ Check enclosed, payable to GSI Publications
☐ Mastercard  ☐ Visa   Expiration Date:_____
Card Number:_____

_____
Cardholder's Signature

**GSI Publications, Inc.**
P.O. Box 746, DeWitt, New York 13214-0746
Phone: (315) 446-4849
Fax: (315) 446-2012

Call us for quantity discounts on large orders.

**GSI**
PUBLICATIONS, INC.